Jem and Jan Win!

by D.M. Longo
illustrated by Hector Borlasca

Target Skill Consonants *Ww*/w/ and *Jj*/j/
High-Frequency Words *green, yellow, blue*

PEARSON
Scott Foresman

Look at Jem!

He can see Jan.

Jem can see a green hat.

Can you see the green hat?

Jem can win it!

Jan can spot a blue cap.
Can Jan hit a blue cap?
Jan can win it!

Jem can see a red cat.

Can you see a red cat?

Jem can win it!

Jan can spot a pink pig.

Can you spot a pink pig?

Jan can win it!

Jem can see a yellow kit!

Will he win it?

Jem can win it!

Look at Jem with Jan!
They can win a lot!